Gods in the Grey City
By: Lenni A.

AF444204

# Gods in the Grey City

Lenni A.

Published by Lenni, 2017.

GODS IN THE GREY CITY

**First edition. November 2, 2017.**

Copyright © 2017 Lenni A..

ISBN: 979-8201569846

Written by Lenni A..

# Also by Lenni A.

**Angel of Flame**
Dahlia
Dahlia: Part 2

**Djinn**
Djinn
Djinn 2: Wendigo

**First Brood: Tales of the Lilim**
First Brood: Dreamhunter
First Brood: Greenhouse
First Brood: Lost Brother

**Fruit of the Dead**
Fruit of the Dead - Season One: Episode One
Fruit of the Dead - Season One: Episode Two

**Go Away Girls**
Go Away Girls: Flight
Go Away Girls: The Mirror


**Standalone**
Gods in the Grey City
Old Soldier
Sacrifice
Sunburn
Winter Boot
Beaverish


Watch for more at www.atthequillsmercy.com/index.html.

# Table of Contents

# Chapter One

When she fell at his feet, he didn't break his stride stepping over her. Like the rest of this place, she is boring. The steady drone of uninteresting peasants, uninteresting merchants beating their uninteresting slaves and pimping their uninteresting wares was only a vague roar around him.

"Hold 'er down!" Yes, nothing special. In a moment she'll scream as she's beaten and cuffed around the ears; as a Muri's ears are very sensitive to pain. She will be subdued, then dragged off to whatever hovel she lives in to be beaten, possibly raped, then put to work when her masters are done with her. Muri slaves are too valuable to kill despite their abundance. No need to stop and look.

The subsequent scream was decidedly male.

Now he stopped.

"She cut off his hand!"

Now he turned.

"She's not supposed to be able to do that! The brand-"

"Obviously doesn't mean a damn thing!"

In between the gawking market goers, he watched three men struggle with the female Muri. He focused on her, the gleaming ribbon of her magic fizzling out and spraying blood in the air. They must have broken her concentration when they wrestled her to the dusty ground. He saw her shirt ride up to expose the brand on her belly; enchanted to prevent the Muri from acting against her masters, a harsh dark scar on the pale, undernourished flesh. Yet, it was ineffective.

Now he walked over.

The Muri struggled against her masters, making it to her feet as he approached. Her magic rippled as she called forth her only defense. He easily wove his way through the gathering crowd, all eyes watching the snarling Muri. The slave's eyes were on her attackers, rage making the vein-blue color as barren as the sand beneath her boots. She paid him no notice as he neared.

Before she fought further, his fist landed firmly on the back of her neck, rendering her unconscious. Her body crumbled to the ground and her ribbon faded away.

"Thank ya kindly, sir. Hope ya don't think us weak for lettin' 'er get the best 'o us there."

He inspected the Muri before looking up at the villager, faceless even as he looked right at him. "I'll buy her." The man murmured, his voice a raspy winter breeze.

The townsman shuddered under the ice of the stranger's whisper. "What for? Ain't got no value. Can't obey for nuthin'. Last guy to try and bed 'er lost more than a hand."

He looked over the townsman's shoulder as some of his equally faceless friends bind up the bleeding stump, and cart off the injured. "One hundred gold for the Muri as she is."

The stranger's fleeting attentions reached the townsman's eyes only when they narrowed in suspicion. "I'd never sell to some nameless fella."

"Ciro. And give me everything she owns. And I mean *everything*."

"Filth don't have possessions."

"I don't care if it's the rise of dirt she sleeps on. I want it." Ciro's yellow eyes bored into the townsman, finally seeing his whole face. Sun tanned and pockmarked, the lack of timely obedience the only vaguely interesting thing about him. Even the protruding belly associated with many sales and little work, was sadly typical.

"One hundred fifty gold and any further negotiations will be poorly received." Ciro dropped the coins into the townsman's hand. Ciro knew the fat man keep quiet. You can get a family of Muri for one hundred fifty gold pieces.

Faceless Townsman shoved the gold into his pockets, and turned to procure what little belongings the Muri must have while Ciro easily flung the blood-spattered slave over his shoulder. A sack containing her possessions was hesitantly placed in his hand, and he turned to the dispersing crowd. He didn't look back.

Ciro ignored the stares as he walked through the streets searching for an inn with an unconscious Muri woman over his shoulder. He only pursed his lips, annoyed the female's face was rubbing on the back of his long coat, doubtlessly spreading saliva all over the expensive hide. He shifted her weight, leaning her away from the hilt against his back and turning her face to the side.

The innkeeper was surprisingly nonplussed when Ciro walked in asking for a room with a table, two chairs, one bed, and a clean washroom for himself and his unconscious companion. He took Ciro's gold and silver coins, gave a key and directions to the room, and went back to his ledger. Efficient. Ciro appreciated that.

The room was well worth his coin. The requested chairs and tables were sturdy and placed close to the window. The bed was clean and freshly made; a pity to drop the filthy Muri on it. Without removing his coat or gloves, he took off her dusty clothes and boots, leaned her against the wall, and dumped them into a basin in the wash room. Ciro flicked a few shavings of the provided soap in with them and vigorously scrubbed the dust and grime from the fabrics.

Ciro spread the Muri's clothes and his gloves on the table while he used a washcloth to clean the dust from his coat without taking it off his back. Only when the last speck was gone did he finally put his new slave into the bath, using a clean cloth to clinically remove the grime from her body. He even went so far as to scrub through the matted hair on her head, the powder blue color finally revealing itself as the filth was washed away. The Muri only groaned when Ciro scrubbed where his fist had left a welt.

Confident she'd heal, Ciro dried her and put her under the linen to keep her warm in the bed while her clothes dried. As she slept, Ciro watched the streets below seated in one of the chairs with his sword in his lap.

# Chapter Two

Ciro rose from the chair at dawn to retrieve food for his slave. Though the Muri didn't appear to have been starved lately, as the woman was all curves and squishy soft, he doubted the men she'd battled had ever given her a decent meal. He balanced the tray of steaming grain, cooked eggs, and thick slices of crisp, fatty meat. He carried enough food and fresh tea for three in one hand as he walked through the silent hallways after rousing a sleepy cook, without clattering the cups on the tray.

Ciro's breathing changed as he approached his room, listening intently to the sounds on the other side. The room and the Muri within it were too quiet. Her breath was calm, slow, preparing for him to enter. Ciro's footsteps did not falter and he slipped his key into the lock without hesitation.

When he opened the door, he ducked the chair aimed at his head, gliding through the movement and crossing the room in three easy strides. The dishes finally made a sound when Ciro placed the tray on the empty table. He almost chuckled. The Muri had awoken, dressed herself in the tattered rags she dared to call a shirt and shorts, and waited to subdue him so she could attempt escape. Her persistence, he found, was something to be admired, as she continued to attack him with the chair.

Once free of the tray, Ciro caught the chair in one hand and pushed the Muri towards the bed with the other with enough force to knock her on her back. While she struggled to her feet,

Ciro shut and locked the door, dropping the key into a coat pocket.

"I did not touch you in any improper way." He said, reading the rage in her eyes. "You have clean clothes and now food. Take advantage of it."

"Liar!" She hissed, launching off the bed. The air twisted as the Muri called forth the only weapon she had, the glimmering ribbon of light forming around her hands.

Ciro drew his blade from his back, a fearsome thick slab of gleaming metal, trapped in form between an axe and a sword. The hooked spikes were spaced perfectly to fit the Muri's narrow neck between them without injury unless she insisted on continuing to move. Lucky for her, she froze.

"Don't." He rasped, meeting her eyes for the first time. Her large orbs were completely filled with a deep blue and they did not waver in their hatred for him when met with the cold intent of his own stare. Her ears flushed bright red with strain as she tried to keep still. "There is nothing about you to raise my interests. I bought you; I washed your filthy clothes and your equally filthy body. I did not molest you or your belongings; which I also purchased. You can believe me or not. Either way, you will now sit in the remaining chair and eat what is provided. If I see a single speck of your magic, I will cut off your hands. Understood?"

The Muri considered carefully before her hands dropped to her sides. Ciro withdrew his weapon but did not return it to the sheath. Instead, he gestured with it towards the table. The smell of fresh food ripped her gaze away from him but she hesitated.

"Eat your fill. I won't take it from you and it isn't drugged."

The Muri's stomach growled loudly, breaking her resolve. As she sat, she tore off a mouth full of meat before snatching up the spoon and bowl of hot grain. She heaped food into her mouth before this strange grey haired man could change his mind. She moved so fast, her boots scuffed the floor and she was seated on her the ends of her hair.

Ciro righted the second chair and sat in front of the door with his weapon in his lap. His face remained neutral as he watched the Muri work her way through the tray. When she paused to reach for a drink, he said "Tell me your name. I refuse to address you as slave."

The Muri glared at him mid swallow and slammed the cup on the table. Her frown made the inked markings on her face crease, the three little triangles becoming broken. "You can't fool me."

Ciro's lips quirked upwards. "Strange name."

She snatched up a slab of bread, ripping it in half. "I know your type." She piled eggs between the steaming pieces. "The other Muri in the slave houses dream and titter about brooding swordsmen with hearts of gold." Her fingers pressed the bread closed to seal in the eggs. "They slay beasts, defeat corrupt lords, and free slaves." She mashed her sandwich together, her raspy voice sliding into a growl. "They were stupid and I find you unimpressive."

"Do you now? Pity. I was impressive enough to buy you; a Muri who can manifest a weapon despite her brand. You are lucky those men did not kill you." Ciro tapped his blade against his breeches. "And you know they would have."

"Better dead than anyone's slave." She said, taking a large bite. "They would have been dead if you haddn't gotten in my way."

"Don't talk with food in your mouth. It's disgusting." Ciro growled. "And I asked your name. I do not like repeating myself."

She looked at the blade in his lap as Ciro turned the handle slowly in his fingers. The light from the window reflected off the blade into her eyes. "Tia." She murmured, swallowing her food carefully before she spoke.

Ciro gave his name with a curt nod to continue eating. He watched Tia grow uncomfortable with his eyes on her but she continued knowing there was nothing to be done about it.

Focusing on her meal, Tia ate until she was sure one more bite would sicken her. Stretching her legs under the table, Ciro caught sight of more thick lines streaming up the Muri's thigh. They were not any marks he recognized and more curved up her arm. "Don't unimpressive strangers need food?" She snarled.

Ciro stood and sheathed his weapon. "I will have to decline such a kind invitation. Take your things and prepare to leave. Since you're mine, you'll be coming with me."

"I am no slave. I refuse to follow you anywhere."

"You wouldn't get down the hallway alone and end up in the exact situation I bought you from or worse. I am headed North. You will follow me willingly or make the journey unconscious over my shoulder. I doubt such an impressive Muri such as you can stand that many blows to the head." Ciro tossed his hair out of his eyes. "And I would get bored of it."

"We'll see how bored you are when I kill you in your sleep." Tia growled, her lips turning further down when Ciro only smiled in response. "You have to sleep sometime."

"Do I?" Ciro returned his chair to the table. "We won't stop at an inn for some time. I suggest you avail yourself of the facilities while you have the chance. I have a long journey and I don't waste much of my coin on places like this. And be quick about it."

Tia cursed her fortunes and sprinted to the washroom.

Ciro watched the streets from the window, the Muri's bag in hand. No one of interest passed his gaze as the first moon set and the sun rose over the city. If she could keep up with him, they would be out of this place by mid-day, just before sunset if she couldn't. When Tia emerged with a clean face and hands, Ciro wordlessly tossed her bag to her and went right to the door. "We have a lot of ground to cover. Do not cause trouble. Keep your eyes on the hem of my coat."

"Like a good little slave, huh? Forget it."

Ciro grabbed Tia by the throat and slammed her against the door. "I would like to get out of this town without having to fight every ten paces." He hissed, Tia scraping desperately at his hand. She could feel the tension in his arm through the thick hide of his coat. His teeth were sharp, straight and bared in abject rage. "You will not be made to fetch or carry. I get what I need to survive on my own and I have no use for you in my bed. You are only required to keep that pride-filled mouth shut and play the role of a docile slave till we reach the forest or I will sew your lips together with hairs from your own head. Understand?"

Without waiting for a reply, Ciro dropped Tia to the floor. She could only answer with gasping coughs. "Get up and follow me. Silently."

Tia swallowed her outrage, snatched up her bag, and did as she was told. There was no way she could fight her way out of the city and Ciro had come across her last attempt to sneak out. He had saved her life in his strange, rude, skinny, yellow-eyed way. Ciro was odd, even for a human. But he passed public scrutiny with his pampered skin and small ears.

*'Damn him, he's right. I can walk out of here if I walk behind him.'*

# Chapter Three

"We'll camp here." Ciro snapped. He'd kept a bruising pace out of the city and into the forest. Tia was nearly limping to follow his tireless strides and collapsed to the ground while Ciro cleared away a place to sleep. "Hope you don't mind sleeping on the ground."

"I've slept in places so horrid; it would put color back in your hair." Tia gasped, leaning her head back against a tree as Ciro prepared stray bits of twig and leaves for a fire. 'How can he still be moving around?'

"Make yourself useful and find more wood for the fire." Ciro muttered, digging a pit with the back of his heel. "And I hear a stream. Get fresh water and a fish for you to eat."

"So much for not being made to fetch." Tia grumbled.

"It's fish or nothing for you. I don't have provisions for two." Ciro slipped a thick tarp from under his coat, leaving Tia to wonder what else he could fit under there. "I was not prepared for impulse buying."

"Filthy jerk." Tia hissed, snatching up her bag and Ciro's water skins and grunting to her feet. Her boots felt like torture devices as she hobbled towards the stream, following the sound of the water.

Ciro listened to the Muri's fading footsteps before dropping a small bundle of kindling into the pit he scored into the ground. He checked the pile, looked up to where Tia had disappeared into the trees. With nothing but silence in her path, he turned his eyes to the kindling and it burst into flame. Ciro studied it a moment before tossing more dry branches into the fire before leaving it to prepare his bedding.

Tia pulled off her boots and eased her burning feet into the gently rolling water, hissing as her skin cooled. She slowed her breathing, sat completely still on the riverbank and watched the water flow. Her large blue eyes waited for movement, for the glimmer of scales, and her ribbon slithered around her neck and shoulders, shimmering in the fading sunlight.

She was still as stone as she waited, having learned patience throughout her slavery. Finding the right moment to strike, run, hide, strike again all the while searching for a way to be free. Fishing was nothing. Ciro was nothing. She could wait for her chance to take care of him, too.

Her ribbon was faster than any stick she could sharpen, spearing a wayward gleam of scale and splash of water at the speed of her thought. Tia lifted a fat, two headed fish and watched it flap its last moments away. A good omen. Patience always paid off in the end, she thought, smiling at the last desperate gasps of her catch.

Ciro held back a smile when Tia returned with an arm full of branches and the fish and water skins draped on her ribbon. "Good catch." He huffed, tossing her a branch to use as a spit. "I'm trusting you know how to clean and cut it."

Tia caught the branch before kneeling by the now roaring fire. Her ribbon shot out, shearing the scales from the fish in quick efficient strokes, and they fell to the earth like glittering tears. Her ribbon also slit the fish to perfectly fit the branch before plunging it into the dirt to roast near the fire. It was then Tia noticed a small iron pot gently bubbling beside the fire. "You had water already." She growled, throwing the swollen water skins at his feet.

"And now we have more." Ciro stowed the skins in his makeshift shelter. "Eat. Then rest. We have a great deal of ground to cover in the morning."

Tia raised a paper thin eyebrow. "Nothing for you again?"

"I had everything I needed while you spent a small eternity at the river. Were you waiting for the fish to grow? Did you sit and feed it 'till it was big enough?"

"You're a horse's ass."

"I'm the horse's front, too. Eat. The shelter is for you. I'll be keeping watch."

Tia nudged the stick holding her fish with the toe of her boot, her hands on her hips in annoyance. "Watch for what?"

"Anything."

"A paranoid horse's ass."

"I expect shit. Eat. Then sleep." Ciro stood and moved away from the fire, leaning against a nearby tree to give his Muri space.

Tia looked around her fish at the shelter. It was a solid structure, metal rods holding tightly stretched animal hides, and thick blankets inside to keep the chill at bay. And not enough room for two. She turned to Ciro to needle more details but his back was to her, arms crossed over his chest and eyes closed. For a moment she considered running. She could wait till he was sleeping deeply, take his belongings, and be too far away to bother chasing after. But something about the way he moved made her certain he would find her and make her more sorry she ran than any other master she'd ever had. He could take her right to her destination much faster and safer than she could manage alone. Tia smiled, fragrant steam rising from her meal as the forest whispered its night song. Once she reached Grey City, she could abandon him under the protection of its walls.

# Chapter Four

Sunlight woke Tia; a nice change of pace from hollered orders or nosey hands. But as her eyes focused it was Ciro's back at the entrance to the shelter which demanded her full attention. She opened her mouth to speak but his hand jerked, the blade coming up to block her mouth. Ciro's chin tightened in warning and Tia nodded. Someone was here.

"I hope you can fight, Muri. I've no taste to be your knight." He hissed at the perfect volume for Tia's high, round ears to catch.

Tia slipped her legs beneath her, a sly grin on her face, ready to spring from the shelter.

"Seven. Armed. Surrounding us."

"Make your move. I'll follow." She whispered.

"Don't get in my way." He growled and Ciro launched from his seated position and towards their assailants so fast, Tia fell back on her behind in shock. Strangling a yelp with a muttered curse, she rolled around the dying embers of their fire and two bloody piles of grey robes. Another fell to Ciro's sword before Tia got to her feet.

Only Ciro's blade was stained with blood, shimmering in the sunlight. Four more grey robes remained; each completely covered save their eyes. Barbed whips were held tightly in their hands. The only color these figures sported was a blood red spiral disk clasping their cloaks to their shoulders. None of them looked at Tia.

Ciro easily ducked the whip coming for his neck, his sword claiming the hand which sent it. The man reared back, taking the loss of his arm with curious silence, and Ciro laid him into the ground with his fist before taking his head as well, leaving the corpse in a crumpled heap.

Tia's wide blue eyes blinked in disbelief. Despite his speed, Tia thought Ciro a short, standoffish oaf, capable of intimidating a slave or some brainless townspeople. What she saw now was skill; pure, lethal, cold, and about to get his ass handed to him if he didn't pay attention.

Two robbed figures advanced on Ciro, going high while the third aimed his whip for Ciro's legs. Tia's ribbon snapped to life as Ciro ducked to save his head, killing the third with a quick thrust to a warm belly. His sword turned to the swatch of grey to his left but not nearly fast enough to take them both. Tia jumped over the dead body, her ribbon flashing in the daylight and splitting open the last grey robbed back. The whip faltered as a clean white spine was exposed to air, missing Ciro completely, leaving her master to carve open the chest of the last.

Tia shook her ribbon very similar in form to how Ciro shook blood off his blade, and allowed it to dissipate, a splatter of blood disrupting the quiet around them. Her new master didn't speak a word as he cleaned the last of the blood off on the cooling body nearest to him, his angular face showing as much annoyance as someone late for a meeting.

"You don't see anything, do you?" Tia muttered, watching Ciro pack up their camp.

"I saw him just fine. Don't think so highly of yourself." Ciro grunted, revealing finally his tent and cookware were rolled tightly in a sack strapped to the small of his back under his thick coat. "Let's get moving."

Tia's eyes went skyward in frustration before kicking the nearest grey robe over. Now she could see the spiral sigil clearly; bone painted with dye and split down the middle with a severe black line. It shivered and rotated and Tia bent closer to watch it.

"They have nothing worth stealing. Move it!" Ciro barked, moving to kick dirt over the black smudge left from their fire. The sigil clicked, turning to follow him.

'*Doesn't really see anything.*' Tia thought, ripping the medallion off the corpse before stepping away. "Don't you want to do something about them?"

"Yes, I want to leave." He tossed her bag and the water skins in the general direction of Tia's hands. She scrambled to catch it, clutching it to her chest and pressing her fingers into the worn canvas to check the contents. Thankfully, nothing was damaged.

With Ciro's back to her, Tia was able to slip the medallion into her bag. None of those men had even looked at Tia. If they were after her master, Tia wanted to know them better.

# Chapter Five

After another full day at a demanding pace and enduring the indignity of being harassed by Ciro while taking care of her business in the bushes, Tia fell to the ground in a pile of sweat and anger, immediately draining her water skin. Ciro calmly set up camp, not a single ash grey hair out of place, breathing evenly as he set up his shelter in record time and left to fill the water skins on his own. "We'll get where I'm going tomorrow."

Tia's head fell back to see the first stars peeking through the darkening sky. She would have smiled knowing she was close to her own goal as well but she kept it to herself. "And where is that?"

Her only answer was his footsteps heading away from her. Tia closed her eyes to concentrate on relaxing her cramping muscles. She blindly reached for her bag, her calloused fingers slipping beneath the tattered flap and pinching the strange medallion to lift it to her line of sight. It clicked and shifted, the black gash in the center turning slowly to follow the direction her new master went.

*'No wonder he's such an edgy bastard. These guys are hunting him.'* She felt something akin to sympathy, familiar with the feeling of dogs at her heels. But he was still her owner, another master. The feeling was bitter and thankfully brief.

"Never forget they believe they own you. You are another chair, a table, a beast of burden." Her elder said. "Never forget a good master is still a master."

"WE LOST THE TEAM SENT to retrieve him."

"By 'lost' you mean Ciro slaughtered them all." Jeshe did not take his yellow eyes away from the sky, pressing his fingers into his narrow chin. He crossed his long legs and the hem of his tunic slid along the animal hide breeches. "He is headed to Grey City."

"There is nothing there." A voice hissed, thin hands sliding up Jeshe's leg. A shimmer of light played on the scaled skin as they scraped at his tunic.

"Go watch him, Erila. Watch him and call me when he arrives at the city." He stroked her wandering fingers with his free hand. "Do good work for me, love."

"Yes, Master." Needle thin teeth flashed before Erila slithered away.

TIA CHEWED LAZILY ON the rib bone of whatever animal Ciro caught while she went to enjoy the lake.

"It's food." He snapped in response to her query, shoving a bowl and spoon Tia had no clue he had into her hands and sulking on the other side of the fire.

Ciro was a confusing son of a bitch. She was ordered to bathe in a lake she never even smelled but Ciro was certain existed. Not only that, he didn't sweat. Tia had yet to see him bathe. Or eat. Or take a sip of water. She cleaned herself till her skin pruned and waited for her clothes to dry without a scrap of interest from her master, who only made a snide remark about how long she took but there was no venom in it. When he threatened to cut off her hands, there was nothing more true in the world. But his mockery was practiced, part of a tailored performance to feign interest in anything other than his own survival.

"You don't belong here." Tia mused, lounging on her side, her creamy blue eyes set firmly on Ciro.

Ciro met the pupil-less eyes. "Neither do you."

"I am Muri. My people are nomads. We don't belong anywhere." Tia snorted, flicking the bright, clean bone into the fire.

"So where are you so determined to go that you thought you could get there alone?" Ciro smirked. "No plan; just thought you'd walk through town like you're some queen."

Tia bit back her sarcasm. "I'm going to Grey City."

"Ah." Ciro chuckled, dropping his hands to his knees. "You think you're gonna rally other escaped slaves. Cute."

Tia grinned, bearing one sharp, little tooth. Grey City belonged to ancient Muri in a time before branded slaves and daily beatings. They were more than free. They were gods. Thanks to the item in her bag, they would be so again. "Yeah, it'll be real cute. Where are you going?"

"Passed there." He huffed and Tia rolled her eyes. "You'll be disappointed trying to bare my soul, Muri."

"I'm not sure your kind have souls." Tia growled.

"All that lives has a soul." Ciro whispered, tossing a twig into the fire. A haze passed over his yellow eyes and he did not look up at his slave.

The Muri's ears flushed bright red in fury and she sat up to glare at her master. "Have you ever heard a Muri woman try to hold in her screams as she's taken while her children watch? Have you heard the sound the infants make when the brand is put to their bellies as soon as the mother-chord is cut? When you smell the burning flesh of a newborn or hear the children wail for the pain of their mother, tell me again you small eared monsters have souls!" Tia spat into the fire and stomped into the tent, her back to her brooding master.

Ciro didn't move; his eyes still on the spot where his slave sat. "A filthy soul is still a soul." He murmured, the leather of his gloves creaking in his clenched fists. "And gods are overrated."

Having this creature with him on his journey amused Ciro, even though he knew what a dangerous distraction she was. A fragile thing in need of food, protection, and carrying some slab of rock she believed would save her people from servitude. He could smell it, taste her vengeful hope the Muri would no longer be slaves. Cute, but futile. It was all futile; all gasping little sparks sputtering against the dark.

And he was no different. On this journey again, sputtering against the dark. Countless times and this one is exactly the same.

Tia grumbled in her sleep. Oh, that had changed. A Muri slave who can injure her captors. Worth the risk to follow her to Grey City. If she did nothing interesting there, he'd leave her with the other Muri. Ciro had no use for slaves. They just cause trouble. He was tired of having to slaughter those grey robed idiots and Tia would only get in the way if she chose to follow him.

# Chapter Six

Tia woke slowly, after both moons had set and the sun was well into morning. Only bird song and the scent of cooked food filled the air. No snotty comments, no orders. Just quiet.

*'Is he dead? Did he abandon me here?'* Both thoughts gave Tia too much relief. But Ciro would not have left food and shelter before taking off and the bastard was too tough die quietly and not wake Tia. She crawled from the tent and saw the sun nearly at its zenith in the sky and Ciro seated by the pot on the fire. "You certainly must be well rested. We should make good time to Grey City."

Tia curled a pump lip in disbelief. "You're gonna escort me there out of the kindness of your heart?"

"One time offer, Muri. Take it or leave it."

Her ears twitched in anger as she stepped from the tent to tell Ciro exactly where he could shove his offer but before she could utter a single word, a silver backed python poised to strike caught Tia's attention. It coiled angrily at her feet, hissing through venom coated fangs.

"Stay still." Ciro muttered, continuing to stir the aromatic contents of the bubbling pot. "She will get bored in a moment and move on to real prey."

Tia watched the snake's eyes, the hollow fangs dripping venom from its open mouth, and knew the snake had no intention of leaving. Tia kept her face calm, waiting for the animal to make a move. They watched each other; the snake hissing in anger, the Muri's ears twitching slightly to gauge the air. Ciro watched them both out of the corner of his eye, curious to see how the Muri would react.

Tia knew the snake would strike. It was in the eyes. But when the snake moved, Tia's ribbon was faster. It came down hard into the ground near Tia's foot, the snake's head slamming into it with a crack so loud, even Ciro cringed. Tia used the ribbon to throw the dazed animal far from the camp then turned to see what Ciro had made for breakfast.

"What?" Tia said when Ciro continued to gawk at her. She spooned food into her mouth as if nearly getting killed by a venomous python was as normal as breathing. "Did you want me to kill it?"

Ciro shuddered at the sight of half chewed stew in Tia's mouth. "She wouldn't have a problem killing you." He looked at the hole in the ground then back to the feasting Muri. "What else can you do with your magic?"

She shrugged, swallowing the last spoonful before filling her bowl again. "Nothing much thanks to the brand. I can carry heavy loads like other slaves." Tia swallowed two more large spoonfuls and Ciro waited patiently for her to continue. "But I can get the ribbon to be as solid as a shield and sharp like a blade. Tried to teach others but no luck." She stopped and looked down at the metal bowl and spoon in her hands. "You didn't have these in town. Where did they come from?"

"I pack efficiently." Ciro peered into the steaming pot, eyes widening at the sight of the scraped clean bottom. He kicked dirt on the fire to allow the pot to cool so he could clean it. "Let's go. No time to lose."

"And how did you know the snake was a she?"

"Move it, Muri!"

"THAT FILTHY CREATURE! That horrible little slave!" Erila hissed, cradling her swollen cheek. "How dare she mar my face!"

"Calm yourself, my pet." Jeshe stroked her head. "You say the Muri did this?"

"With that graceless ribbon of hers. And without her Master's orders! Disobedient peasant chaff!"

Jeshe stood from his table, the wood creaking as he stretched to his full height. Erila scooted away from him, holding her jaw in her clawed hands. "A Muri who harmed another without permission from her master." He began to pace. "And you are sure he owns her?"

"Y-yes, Master. I heard them talking and Ciro said he owned her."

"And she is still branded?"

"She said as much but I couldn't see." She whimpered, stroking a long but cracked fang. "She is an aberration, Master. Let me kill her!"

"Ciro first, my love." Jeshe moved to the window, leaning against the stone. He eyed the approaching storm with cold eyes. "Once we get him, you can do what you wish with the Muri."

Erila smiled carefully around her aching jaw, midnight black hair falling into her face.

# Chapter Seven

Ciro only raised an eyebrow when he saw just how many escaped Muri were camped outside Grey City. The tents extended so far from the city walls; they were only a stone shadow in the distance and nearly blotted out by cooking fires.

"Finally." Tia gasped, wiping sweat from her brow with the back of her hand. The muscles in her thighs and calves vibrated and twitched but the sight of her fellow Muri gave her angry appendages reason to continue a few steps further. Those moth-eaten tents with patched tarps were palaces to Tia. "You may want to stay close to me, Ciro." She held her pack close to her chest. "The guards take to outsiders exactly like you'd think."

Two arrows landed with decisive aim right in front of Ciro's toes. "I can see that." He smirked.

"Stop! He's -" Alright? Tolerable? "Not trouble!" Tia screamed at the trees and three male Muri jumped down from their posts in the branches. "You wouldn't be surprised at how many humans would love to find this place." Tia couldn't believe she was making excuses for her people but she had to be sure Ciro wouldn't attack.

Ciro only grunted in agreement, uncomfortable with so many bright, pupil-less eyes watching him.

"You bring this stranger here? Tia, what are you thinking!?" The tallest one snorted down at her and Ciro smiled when Tia cut him off with a mere look but spoke for good measure.

"He's a jerk but this jerk helped me get here. You can trust him not to betray our location because he doesn't give a shit about anyone but himself." Tia spun on her heel and walked towards the nearest cluster of tents. Ciro thought it wise to follow her. He grinned at the taller Muri and did his best not to laugh under his breath.

The crossbows the males carried were so worn; they seemed more likely to crumble in their hands than hit a target. The tents were in the same condition, patched and sewn multiple times and perched precariously near small fires. The misshapen shelters even leaned against the walls of the city. Humans shunned this place, fearing the abandoned city. Whatever lay within was fully sealed, an ideal place for fleeing slaves far from any other villages and protected by the wall from whatever wailed on the other side of it.

'*How can the Muri not hear it? Especially with those big ears.*' Ciro thought. The churning of the lost souls, their shuddering sighs, their hunger… It all grated on Ciro right down to the bone. He should not be here so close to them. Not just for the sake of the freed slaves or the lost ones who writhe behind the wall. The Muri may not hear them or know what they say, but Ciro knew and his pursuers would come here and disturb them further if they weren't here already. He needed to be on his way; and soon.

His yellow eyes flared and he bit the inside of his cheek to keep the tension from the suspicious eyes of the Muri flanking him and watching for any excuse to make a big mistake and restrain Ciro in any way. His own Muri was walking obliviously ahead of the whole group, greeting other Muri as she strode by. Familiar surroundings put a spring in her step, increased blood flow to her raised ears to make them blush pink when before they were pale and slightly folded with frustration. She lifted a young Muri boy up to nuzzle her nose with his. The boy's belly was pristine; likely he was born here at the wall.

A sharp jab shoved Ciro forward. "Keep your eyes off our young, human." The tallest male hissed.

"'Our young?' He must not be yours." Ciro laughed, assessing the much taller man. He and all the others were clothed in patched together scraps of cloth. "Figures."

"Castor!" Tia barked when Castor went to use his weapon. She set the boy down and Ciro watched him scamper off to a pair of rightly concerned parents and a gaggle of siblings. "I wouldn't. You like your limbs, right?"

Castor fixed his blue eyes on Tia before nearing her so he thought Ciro couldn't hear him. "You would choose this human? A master who bought you like some horse?"

Tia leaned around him, looked Ciro in the eyes, then craned her neck to look at Castor. "If he wanted it, he wouldn't know what do to with it." Tia's voice desired no privacy or held a single ounce of shame. She was truly a woman without couth. "And neither would you."

Castor didn't dare make a move when she turned her back to him but Ciro could feel his covetous gaze on her flesh, on the rise of her backside as it stretched the threads of the tattered rags wore. Ciro was tempted to tease further about what would happen to the man if he refused to let a wild spirit like that one be. But boredom set in once again. In the morning, he would leave the foolish Castor to his ill fated romance.

# Chapter Eight

The old Muri hunched over the wrapped totem, running his fingers over the cloth. He took his time mapping the object before removing the binding. "I am impressed with you, Tia." He whispered, his voice like clay pots being ground into the dirt. "Do you know if this will aid us in overcoming the brand?"

"Not sure, Safuc." Tia leaned back on one of the poles holding up the tent. "But it scares the humans. Therefore, I want it." She breathed in the incense mingling with the scent of whatever the hunters caught before the sun set. The familiarity relaxed her after being so far from her people for so long.

Safuc laughed wetly, unwrapping the tattered cloth to feel the smooth totem, his gnarled fingers seeing what his clouded eyes could not. His wrinkled ears flicked front in thought. "I don't understand these carvings. But given time and better eyes than mine, we will puzzle it out."

"I'm tired of waiting" Tia growled. "I'm tired of being beaten and whored out to the humans; tired of singed flesh and scars. I want to be free."

Safuc handed the tablet and it's wrappings to Tia to put together, clucking his tongue. "Times have been far worse. Now there is a place for us to run when we flee. The humans will not dare come to Grey City."

"I've seen their hate overcome fear. They will come. We will not be safe here forever." Tia wrapped the tablet firmly and put it back in her bag, nodding gently as she turned to leave. When she exited, Castor blocked her path to her own shelter.

"Why did you bring him back here?" He hissed, glowering down at the much shorter female.

"Oh, I dunno. I've always wanted a pet." Tia shouldered him aside. "He's already been housebroken, too. What a find."

Castor held Tia's arm in a strong hand and was immediately wrapped from the neck up in her ribbon. She used her magic to pin Castor to the ground then straddled his chest, trapping his arms with her knees.

"Put your hand on me again and you will be the first Muri I castrate." When Castor finally choked out a plea for mercy, Tia rose and left him sputtering for air on the ground; her ribbon following behind her.

"Don't be foolish, Castor." Safuc murmured, a thin attendant holding open the tent flap.

"She dallies with that human!" Castor had the good sense to allow shame to color his face and ears as other Muri watched him.

Safuc shook his head, wisps of white hair coming free from the leather thong at his neck to brush his high, round ears. "Tia desires only freedom. Leave her be before she decides you are an obstacle to her goals."

"But, Safuc -"

"All her life she has worked and sacrificed for all of us. Do not shame her by forcing your selfish desires upon her."

Castor picked himself up and inclined his head to the elder Muri; but said not a single word as he stormed off.

TIA WISHED FOR THE satisfaction of a door slam when she pinned her tent flap closed. She dragged her hand over her face and scowled when she found it trembling.

"You fear him?" Ciro's voice gave Tia only a small start before she reasoned there was no other place he could be in camp. He would find it too boring to be anywhere else.

"Why the hell are you in my tent?"

"You could turn him into carrion before he could blink." Ciro continued without hesitation, stroking his smooth chin with gloved fingers. "He's a strong enough male, decent face, tall and all stupid with muscle. Not that you need protecting, but he would make a decent enough distraction for your enemies."

"Get out." Tia moaned, gripping the stone slab to her chest. "You are annoying and I am tired."

Ciro was undeterred. "He's as dumb as dirt but his desire for you is obvious."

"I do not trust the desires of men!" Tia screamed, tempted to throw the stone slab at her intruder if it would shut his mouth.

"If its females you desire, simply tell him."

"I desire freedom!" Tia ground her teeth, hissing at Ciro before snatching a neat bundle of fabric and a small bag of scentless scraps of soap. "And solitude." She said, releasing the ties and leaving Ciro alone.

Only when the tent flap stilled did Ciro stop stroking his chin and stand, chuckling under his breath. The Muri was fun to mess with but he would have to move on. But when he slipped out of Tia's tent and saw Castor following her, Ciro was simply too curious and too cautious to allow his Muri to be left alone with Castor.

TIA STRIPPED AND IMMERSED herself in the nearest warm pool of water. She leaned on the steaming rocks and unwrapped her prize, looking to get an eyeful before she lost it to the scholars; Muri smarter than she, having studied what bits of information gleaned from the scraps of scrolls and broken pottery left outside the city walls. She ran her damp fingers on the strange, swirling writing and wished it would somehow speak to her. If she traced them, would it call to her brand? Would it tell her how to remove it from her people and take their birthright as free beings?

The slab did as stone does; remain cold and silent, patiently taking her touch.

Disgusted with herself, Tia covered the totem and leaned back to bathe. She scrubbed herself clean of her childish hopes and the grit of all her travel. The warm water eased her aches and Tia drenched her clothes as well to make herself presentable to turn over the slab. She couldn't shame herself by appearing grimy.

CASTOR WATCHED TIA nearly abuse her skin in the name of cleanliness. Water beaded on her flesh, making even her scars and tattoos glisten like jewels. He'd called her crazy when Tia had paid to have more marks carved into her thigh, arm, and cheek – the vivid blue swaths of color matching the eyes of all Muri.

"I can control these." She'd snarled at him when he demanded she at least not mark her face. "Every time one of those humans dare call me 'slave,' my tattoos will remind them I make my own choices."

"You can almost smell her, can't you?"

Castor nearly fell from the tree branch he was perched upon but regained his footing to see Ciro lounging in the same tree above him. "Get away from here, human."

"You Muri have big ears and Tia isn't as stupid as you. She'll hear you if you don't keep it down." Ciro adjusted his coat and crossed his legs.

"Why do you spy on our women?" Castor gripped the dagger in his belt.

"I'm spying on you and watching out for my investment. I did purchase her, after all." Ciro's lip curled in amusement at the familiar sound of metal sliding against a sheath. "Too easy with that temper. You'll never win her and you'll get yourself killed." He waved a gloved hand. "Don't let me interrupt you. Feel free to continue your voyeurism."

Castor put his weapon away but did not turn his back to watch Tia. "You had no need to follow her to Grey City. Why do you stay?"

"Boredom." Ciro shrugged his shoulders, the custom made scabbard scraping the wet bark. "A Muri who can manifest is a rare treat. I want to see how it plays out."

"You sicken me." Castor mumbled.

"Says the big eared pervert spying on naked women in his spare ti-" Ciro shot to his feet, drawing his weapon and leaping to Castor's back. His gloved hand came down hard on the male Muri's mouth, smothering the indignant grunts. "Silence."

Ciro watched Tia clean her hair, the bulk of the ice blue strands falling into her eyes. She didn't see the python winding towards her, slithering atop the surface of the water. The serpent raised her head, slowly changing in form to reveal the scaled torso of a woman with dripping fangs in a sneer of pure rage.

Leaving Castor to sputter in confusion, Ciro launched from the tree branch and slammed feet first into the snake woman. Tia didn't bother to cover herself and in a slew of hair-curling foul language, she conjured her ribbon to shield any incoming attacks, pushing her hair from her eyes.

"Ciro! What in all the realms are you doing!?"

"I don't think that snake you spared thinks you did her a favor." Ciro brandished his blade at the writhing scales. "I should have recognized you before, Erila. Now, don't be stupid and tell your master you never found me or this place."

Tia gaped. "You know her!?" She screeched.

Before Ciro could answer, Erila's coils knocked him into the water sending up a wave. Tia had to use her ribbon to shield herself as she scrambled to keep her footing.

*'Well, she's gotten faster.'* Ciro thought, as he struggled to gain his footing. Water pushed his grey hair into his eyes and turned his coat into a heavy weight on his back. Swatting away the hair revealed a sight he never thought would be possible: A naked Muri battling an enraged snake woman with the Muri holding her own. Tia blocked the striking coils with her ribbon, the scales hitting with a wet thrump as they were deflected and parried instantly with a swath of sharp magic. Erila lost strips of scale to

the diminutive Muri, fueling the snake woman's rage and making her sloppy.

Ciro launched from the water, his legs propelling him high enough to land on a section of Erila's writhing coils close to her torso. He buried the hooks of his blade deep into her flesh to keep hold. "Back away, Muri!" He screamed.

"Like hell." Tia spat, stealing Ciro's idea of using her weapon to climb up the twisted, snarling Erila. Several of Castor's arrows served as a distraction as black red blood spattered from the wounds Tia inflicted riding her ribbon up the coils. It left deep gashes in its wake and supported Tia on the flat edge.

"You are mad." Ciro grumbled, swinging his feet up to strike a heel into Erila's chin. She screeched in agony, the impact cracking an already weakened fang. The serpent woman snatched the leg that struck her, sinking remaining her fang through Ciro's breeches.

Bellowing in pain, Ciro pinned Erila's wrists with his legs and his Muri speared her through the chest. Tia's ribbon knocked a spiral medallion off of Erila's neck and as she reared back to scream, Ciro cut off her head.

The trio tumbled down in a chaotic heap too jumbled for Castor to make sense of. He dropped his crossbow screaming out for Tia as he ran into the water. He pulled her sputtering form to land releasing her only when she tried to swear and only water burbled from her lips.

"What was that?" She gasped, curling around the burn of aching lungs.

Castor draped the cloth Tia brought with her over her shoulders as she began to shiver, then turned back to the water.

"I've never seen a creature like that." His skin paled as the water stilled. "They're gone."

Tia tried to stand but her legs, unfamiliar with climbing giant monsters, buckled from the exhaustion. Cursing her weakness, she coughed. "What do you mean 'gone?'"

"Gone, Tia. There is nothing in the water." Castor's hands balled into fists. "Not even blood."

This time, Tia forced her legs to do her bidding, wrapping the tablet with more care than her naked body. "Gather everyone and set up extra guard. I'll track him down."

"Why?"

"You think the snake woman was the only one to come after Ciro?" Tia grabbed her bag and shoved the tabled into Castor's hands. "Take this to the scholars. Tell them what happened."

"Tia?!"

"Castor, I'm not going to listen to what you or anyone says. So, let's just skip the lecture so I can do what I please, alright?" Tia picked up her soaked clothes and headed for her tent. "And stop staring at me while I'm naked."

Castor sighed, rubbing his face before he did as he was told.

# Chapter Nine

Ciro had forgotten cold. He remembered the concept, knew other creatures experienced the sensation, but to have ice fill his veins and his very being cry out for sleep as his body shivered in a desperate bid for warmth was new.

"Erila's venom." Jeshe mused, kicking the coils from Ciro's body. "An effective paralytic, even against someone like you."

Ciro couldn't manage the exasperated sigh the situation called for. It irked him to have his coat rumbled by being prone on the floor. When Jeshe used his boot heel to push Ciro onto his back, Ciro decided Jeshe's scalp would certainly buff out any scratches.

"She was a very rare talent. Not many can shape shift as fast as she could. Hard to replace. But I'll make do." Jeshe gifted Ciro with a calculating leer which made Ciro's lips twitch into a frown.

Distantly, Jeshe continued talking but Ciro's yellow eyes took stock of his situation. His body was burning through the venom slowly so it would be awhile before Ciro could escape. Jeshe couldn't kill him, leaving boredom as Ciro's only real threat while still in the stone walls. He could hear the winds howling outside and liberal strikes of lightning beating the ground. Likely no shelter for miles which would make things interesting-

"Worried about your Muri?"

Oh, yeah. Her.

"I believe she is on her way to us. A loyal Muri come to rescue her master? Another rare thing. I see why you stopped to purchase her." Jeshe was very boring and Ciro would have tapped an impatient foot were he capable.

Then a blade the color of daybreak, vivid red and orange, descended into Ciro's line of sight.

"We will go to meet her, yes? We can test out my trinket and all your power will be mine."

Another new sensation filled Ciro. Panic. It tasted awful.

"OF COURSE YOU WOULD be in there. Why in all the hells would you be somewhere that made sense?" Tia growled, wishing Ciro were there to be cursed at in person.

The red spiral shuddered and the black gash pointed right at the gates of Grey City, clicking as if insisting Ciro was beyond the walls of the abandoned city.

"Don't do it, Tia." Castor, trailed by Safuc and his attendant. "Let the human go to his fate."

"We are not to cross the wall!" Safuc had to lean on his cane as he trembled with the thought of what Tia was about to do.

"Castor, you tattletale." Tia growled, ignoring them all and walking up to the crumbling stone gates. "After that snake vanished, she took Ciro with her and this thing," Tia waved the medallion in the air with her thumb and forefinger, the black gash clicking in protest. "Says he's in Grey City. None of you are the least bit curious how she breached the walls without opening them? Or how he's survived inside?"

"No." Castor said firmly, his brows lowering in frustration. "It is not for us to disturb the city. Especially for the sake of a human."

Tia snorted. "Not for you, maybe. But I'm not scared of the songs beyond the wall." Ignoring the horrified gasps of the males behind her, Tia put her palm right on the unknown carvings.

Nothing happened.

"Don't you do this!" Castor hollered.

"Either shut up or help me open this gods forsaken door!" Tia screeched. Her temper in control of her ribbon, she slammed it against the seal, cursing so thoroughly, Safuc coughed and his attendant blushed all the way to the curve of his round ears.

A crowd began to gather, aghast Tia would dare to touch the wall and watching her pound on it with her ribbon. "I know you're back there, you ass! You better not think you can hide form me! I still owe you for the lump on my head!" She screamed, throwing the spiral medallion at the wall. When it didn't shatter, Tia's shoulders slumped.

"Tia," Castor kept his distance. "Let it go."

"Never." She rasped.

The stone doors groaned and every Muri but Tia took a step back. Tia charged forward as the stone gates parted.

"No!" Castor started after her but was too slow to stop her from slipping between the gates the moment a large enough space was available. The ground shook with the force of the stone rumbling through the motions despite years of no movement. Dust and pebbles rained down on Castor before he lunged for the opening.

"What are you doing?" Safuc pulled on Castor's tunic, nearly ripping the fragile garment.

"You heard her! We can either help or get out of the way." Castor squeezed the old Muri's hand gently, reassuring him. "I won't let her face what's beyond the wall alone."

"Stubborn young ones." Safuc motioned to his attendant who dutifully took the old Muri's arm and placed it around Castor's elbow. "Lead on then. Satisfy this old one's curiosity."

Castor shook his head, certain that in his prime Safuc had been as much or more trouble than Tia. The thought earned a deep shudder of fear before the two of them walked between the gates.

TIA FELT THE GREY HAZE part around her as she jogged further into the city searching for some sign of Ciro or Erila. The calm whispering in the fog kept her lips tightly shut against the curses begging to come out. Nothing could be seen beyond the two-foot circle of clear air around Tia's body, everything around her a muted soup, no sign of anything or anyone.

As she walked, dark clouds distinguished themselves from the grey muck and the spiral clicked in excitement. Tia broke into a punishing run. When she was sure she would step into a storm, her ribbon forming to protect against the rain, she was momentarily blinded by intense sunlight. She skidded to a halt, a cloud of dust swirling around her feet. Within the walls, within the mists of Grey City was a complete desert amid the forests surrounding the wall.

"What in all the-"

Tia was denied the pleasures of her foul mouth by Castor slamming into her back. The two rolled into the light, quickly becoming covered in dirt.

"Castor, you ass! Get off me!" Tia flailed till the male rolled away. "Why did you follow me!?"

"You said to shut up or help." Castor rose and dusted himself off. "We picked help."

"We? Are you kidding me!?"

"No. He most certainly is not, Tia." Safuc's nearly blind eyes were the only ones to be unfazed by the burst of sunlight beating down upon them. Castor used his ribbon to shield his eyes. "That was foolish, child."

"Yet you came." Tia planted her fists on her hips above the roll of fabric keeping the threadbare shorts on. "Now get out of sight. Something's not right."

"I hear it." Safuc leaned hard on the Muri escorting him. "The voices from the mist are all singing in unison."

A lone figure ambled towards them, his shuffling feet leaving a trail of dust in his wake. Another followed, flanked by nothing but an angry red glow.

"Castor, take Safuc and hide behind the dunes. If that snake is there, she's too dangerous to fight with you all close to me."

"Tia." Castor hissed.

"Go! Before she gets here!" Tia moved away from the rise in the sand to keep the focus on her and away from the Muri who couldn't defend themselves with their magic.

As the figure neared, Tia recognized the trail of ash-grey hair unique to Ciro. She stepped forward, insults on her tongue but they died immediately at the sight of him. The signature coat and gloves were gone and Ciro was unarmed. Red lines coiled over his skin, up his hands, across his shoulders and interlocking over his bare chest. As he approached, Tia saw the man behind Ciro wielding a blade with the horrid red glow.

Ciro's yellow eyes were blank, his face completely placid. He only stopped walking when the stranger behind him did.

"Well, your Muri did come for you. Aren't you glad, Ciro?"

Ciro didn't move.

"You will have to forgive my servant's rudeness, slave. Just because you are Muri doesn't mean he can be rude." Jeshe lifted the dagger. "Bow nicely to the female, Ciro."

Without blinking, Ciro bent at the waist, his eyes never looking at her, and stood straight in a smooth motion.

"I should thank you for bringing him to me, Muri. He is a fitting replacement for my dear departed Erila."

*'The snake woman is dead.'* Tia set a mask of boredom firmly on her face despite the hammering in her chest. "Well, I've come to fetch him. Busy tending to Master, you see."

Smirking, Jeshe inclined his head and Ciro pounced like a wild animal, lifting Tia from the ground in one powerful hand around her neck.

*'Ah, gotta love familiar ground.'* Tia did her best not to struggle, holding on to Ciro's arm which was so tight with muscle, she knew it was futile to pull away.

"You don't realize who bought you, slave!" Jeshe cackled. "You should be thanking me for keeping him on a leash! Ciro is not human. He is a god of fire descendant to pass judgment on this world." Jeshe circled them, ignoring Tia's gasps for breath. "He travels from pole to pole, assesses what lives and if it does not please him, Ciro burns the world clean to start again." He put his lips to Tia's ear, her struggles keeping Jeshe's attention as Castor made to help her. Safuc's attendant held him back. "Think of all the lives he's taken. Billions of souls gone and he thought nothing of it. Except for you."

When Tia's face turned blue, Jeshe tapped a finger on Ciro's arm. Ciro dropped her, leaving Tia to cough and gasp on the ground. "A Muri who can do battle with her magic. A rarity indeed." He mused, pacing around them both. "With Ciro under my control, we could free your people from bondage and return them to their former splendor."

Tia scowled at him, her glare telling Jeshe what she thought of his offer. "What would you know of our splendor?"

Jeshe laughed and pointed to the hissing grey mist circling them, kept at bay by a clear sky and powerful sunlight. "The Muri lived here centuries ago. A small but powerful nation using their magics at will. A bit too much will." The souls in the mist wailed and Tia warred with the urge to clamp her hands over her ears. "They lost themselves in the power, destroyed themselves and the entire city. Survivors sealed the lost souls in and fearful humans sealed their power. And the rest," Jeshe pointed at Tia's brand. "Is history."

Roaring, Tia went to claim that flippant finger with her ribbon, wondering what sort of necklace she would make with the bones but Ciro caught the ribbon in his hand before Tia could claim her prize. Her eyes met his; hot furious blue to blank yellow cold.

"Pity. But I appreciate a firm answer. We could have done great things, Muri." Jeshe turned the blade in his hand, admiring the light. "Kill her."

There was no emotion in Ciro's face when his fists came at her, the strikes barely held back by the swift motions of Tia's ribbon. Tia prayed Castor wouldn't be stupid enough to try and interfere. Unarmed and unable to use his ribbon in battle, he would be in worse shape than Tia, who could feel the force in Ciro's fists rattling her body and struggled to match his speed.

In the end, her ribbon was only as fast as her own mental strength and Ciro knocked her across the rough terrain. Grunting in pain, Tia struggled to her feet, spitting blood from a loose tooth and split lip in Jeshe's general direction. "Even as a puppet, he still hits like a kid."

Her vision swam as Ciro continued his assault, his limbs flying faster and harder than any human being could possibly muster and earning Tia more bruises and cracked bones for her trouble. Ciro's face and neck were sliced with shallow wounds but he didn't flinch when they were inflicted nor when wind blew sand inside them.

"Stop playing with her, servant." Jeshe feigned a yawn, tapping his palm with the flame colored blade. "We have much to do. Kill the slave."

"No!" Castor leaped from his hiding place, his ribbon a streak of light in his wake. He was able to block Ciro's deadly strike to Tia's head, the fist hitting the light with a sickening crack.

"You *idiot*!" Tia screamed, smoothly pulling Castor behind her to spear Ciro through the shoulder. Her ribbon left a clean hole, spraying Ciro's bright red blood as a cover, the ribbon sailing through Ciro's flesh to knock the blade from Jeshe's hand.

Ciro went unfazed by the wound, snatching up Tia's wrist and knocking Castor aside in the same quick stride. With her concentration broken along with her wrist, Tia's ribbon dissipated. Ciro used Tia's arm to slam her hard into the ground, her head leaving a gash in the dirt and oozing blood.

Castor had no breath to scream her name. His eyes gaped at the sight of her motionless, blood pooling around her and Ciro stepping back to his master with his blank yellow gaze on Tia's body.

"Good." Jeshe retrieved the blade and turned on his heel towards the gate. "A pity though. A strong female like that gone to waste. Come we have work to do." He took two steps and stopped, puzzled by the lack of Ciro's footfalls behind him. He squeezed the hilt of the blade. "Come!"

Ciro's shoulders twitched but he did not obey. His chin went down to his chest, eyes stuck on the body of his Muri. Fat tears rolled from his eyes, steaming when they hit his super-heated cheeks.

Jeshe sighed. "Even an enslaved god gives me trouble." He huffed, striding up to Ciro and collecting blood from the oozing shoulder wound with the tip of the blade. It pulsed with the fire god's heart once before going completely dark.

"What?" Jeshe did not feel the wind pick up around him. "If this thing is broken, I will use it to carve out your heart." He growled at Ciro, sneering down at the shorter man.

The sun went out. The grey mist swarmed Tia's body, which rose with the force of the wailing souls and glowed bright to replace the sun's light. The howling glow crawled across her skin burning away at her brand. It hissed and writhed on the seal of her magic, devouring it till her belly was clean. Her eyes opened, bright feral blue, and the wind flared hot and angry to instantly dry the moisture on Ciro's face and searing Jeshe's skin.

Jeshe watched the Muri in full on panic, pushing Ciro towards her. "Kill her! Kill the slave!" He screamed and Ciro obeyed, his skin glowing red with heat as he attacked with his hands and feet. Tia's ribbon blocked every strike with effortless precision as she stood unmoving in the center of a storm of wailing souls.

"Tia!" Castor screamed, trying to shield the elder from the howling winds. "End this! We can't take much more!"

*'Cover yourselves.'* One and many voices whispered to Castor and he pushed his concentration to the limit to form a dome to protect them. It shuddered with the force of the rage around them.

The winds shoved Ciro back and trapped him against Jeshe, who stumbled while Ciro remained on his feet and crouched to face the glowing Muri at the center of the horrid storm. Their eyes met again and Tia screamed the voices of all the souls, light enveloping the desert battlefield in blinding white, wiping it clean in a ball of pure pain and rage.

# Chapter Ten

Tia woke alone on her back in what looked like her own tent to the sounds of excited chatter. She rubbed her face, finding every muscle sore and skin dry from dehydration. Her belly growled and Tia growled back, ignoring her aches as she sat up.

"I wondered if you'd sleep all day. Lazy Muri."

Tia groaned. "Ciro, I had the most marvelous dream. I was beating the crap out of you."

When she turned toward the chuckling man, she saw him leaning on the main pole of her tent without his signature coat or gloves. When he caught her questioning gaze on his marks, Ciro shrugged. "No point in hiding them now. All the Muri know what I am." He rose to his feet with a slow grace he usually saved for his sword play. "You were sleeping for a week. Get off your fat ass and speak to your people." He smiled before turning to leave her alone.

When Tia took better stock of her surroundings, she saw a tray of food waiting for her and her clothes neatly folded at the foot of her mat. Tia looked down at her bare breasts. "Caught naked by that horse's ass again." She groaned and her stomach echoed her. "Oh, knock it off." She glared down at her stomach and gasped. The world spun and Tia forgot how to breathe. Trembling fingers touched her belly in disbelief. She was free. The brand was gone.

Tia rubbed her flesh, enjoying the smooth, unscarred skin. Every old wound was gone save the tattoos. Hearing voices outside her tent, she reluctantly rolled her sore body from her mat and shrugged into her clothes, holding a hot slice of sweet cake in her mouth as she tugged her boots onto her feet. She was still chewing when she walked out of her tent using her arm to shield her eyes from the sun. Then the cheers rang out and Tia's head throbbed.

"Tia!" Castor ran to her side, smiling at the sour expression he was greeted with when he steadied her. "Everyone's glad to see you're alright. You slept through the entire relocation."

"What?" Tia mumbled, crumbs slipping into her shirt and her blue eyes narrowing in a perfect storm of confusion and annoyance.

"You cleared out the souls from Grey City. So, of course we moved everyone inside the walls." Castor waved his hand to draw Tia's attention to the other Muri busily going about their day between waving and cheering for Tia.

"Are you sure it's safe?" Tia didn't remember anything after getting her head pounded into the ground by Ciro and it hurt to try and remember anymore.

"Safe for now." Ah, speak of the devil. Ciro stood with his hip cocked to one side and his naked blade in a tight fist, the blunt end resting across his shoulders. "Come with me. You need to see this." Without waiting for a reply, he turned on his heel expecting her to follow.

"I'm gonna kill him." Tia growled, stomping after him. Castor only shook his head and headed towards a group of other males clearing land for crops.

Ciro lead Tia across the dusty landscape to a marble tower far from camp, trudging at a pace Tia thought impossible for such a short human.

'*But he's not exactly human.*' She reminded herself as she trotted behind him. "So, fire god, eh?"

"Yes." Ciro stopped at the archway and turned to face her. "It's why I don't sweat, don't sleep, and why I am perpetually bored."

"And why you had those metal dishes in the forest but no flint." Tia glanced at Ciro's hands. "You can forge rock into metal."

Ciro grinned. "Not as dumb as I thought, Muri." He quipped and turned to enter the tower. "Jeshe lived here." He explained as they walked the zigzagging staircases to the top. "Since you killed him, you should have it."

When they reached the top, Tia took a moment to catch her breath. Doubled over panting, her arms propping her up on her knees, Tia saw the lavish bed and single deck in the large room. It took up the entire width of the building and Tia had never had so much space to herself. It was all easily three times the size of her tent or more. The furniture would have to go. Tia didn't want to sleep on the same bed as Jeshe.

"Look." Ciro curtly pointed out onto the terrace and Tia joined him on it. "Jeshe somehow kept the souls at bay while living here. But you took care of that. Now, Grey City is yours." Ciro handed Tia the blade Jeshe used to control him, now faded and clear as if made of glass. He held it out to her holding it by the blade. "As is this."

"Why are you giving this to me?" Tia put her fists on her hips, staring at Ciro in complete disbelief. "Why not destroy it?"

"Can't." Ciro's eyes remained on the landscape and he wouldn't take back the dagger. "And you are such an idiot; I know you won't use it."

Snorting, Tia took the dagger by the hilt. "I should just jam it down your throat."

"Probably." Ciro muttered. "You started something here, Muri. The humans saw the light coming from you. They won't like the idea of a city full of pissed off runaway slaves lead by an unbranded, god-like female."

"I'm no leader."

"You better be. Because there will be war."

"Shit." Tia leaned on the terrace, rubbing fatigue from her face. "You better leave then. They won't take kindly to a descendent god, either."

"And miss this? A showdown between free Muri and humans? No chance, Muri."

Tia looked out at Grey City, for now just a collection of quickly assembled tents and piles of stone to make permanent housing later. Other Muri still poured through the gates and Safuc worked with the scholars to bring water into the city. Children played while their parents carried their life's possessions with their ribbons. The city was filled with happy work, the hopeful sounds of a new future.

"We'll give 'em hell." Tia vowed.

"Sure will, Tia."

She didn't remark on the use of her name. They only watched Tia's people settle into their new home.

End

# Don't miss out!

Visit the website below and you can sign up to receive emails whenever Lenni A. publishes a new book. There's no charge and no obligation.

https://books2read.com/r/B-A-ZHQD-WDVP

BOOKS 2 READ

Connecting independent readers to independent writers.

Did you love *Gods in the Grey City*? Then you should read *Djinn*[1] by Lenni A.!

Missy is bound to a djinn who insists on calling himself Todd. He lives with her, follows her to work, and generally makes a nuisance of himself. Until the day a mute child falls literally into Todd's lap needing their help. This quick misadventure threatens to reveal secrets Missy has tried hard to conceal and secrets Todd is all too eager to tell.

Read more at www.atthequillsmercy.com/index.html.

---

1. https://books2read.com/u/mdNjvZ

2. https://books2read.com/u/mdNjvZ

# Also by Lenni A.

**Angel of Flame**
Dahlia
Dahlia: Part 2

**Djinn**
Djinn
Djinn 2: Wendigo

**First Brood: Tales of the Lilim**
First Brood: Dreamhunter
First Brood: Greenhouse
First Brood: Lost Brother

**Fruit of the Dead**
Fruit of the Dead - Season One: Episode One
Fruit of the Dead - Season One: Episode Two

Watch for more at www.atthequillsmercy.com/index.html.

# About the Author

Lenni is the pen-name for a librarian with a wild imagination. She loves reading, writing, drawing, baking, and not nearly enough hours in the day to do all these things. She has been writing since she can hold a pen and reading since she could hold a book. You can see her full body of work at www.atthequillsmercy.com and check out her blog over at www.literaryloon.com.

Read more at www.atthequillsmercy.com/index.html.

# About the Publisher

www.ingramcontent.com/pod-product-compliance
Lightning Source LLC
Chambersburg PA
CBHW020133180726
47992CB00022B/2914